MONSTER FART WARS:

FARTS VS. BURPS

Book 1

A.M. SHAH

Published by 99 Pages or Less Publishing, LLC
Miami, FL
For inquiries email: info@99pagesorless.com

Printed in the United States of America
10 9 8 7 6 5 4 3 2 1

Cover Illustration by: Pedro Demetriou
Typesetting by: Mandi Cofer

Library of Congress Cataloging-in-Publication Data is available for this title.

Library of Congress Control Number: 2016920972

ISBN: 978-1-943684-51-9 (hc); ISBN: 978-1-943684-50-2 (sc);
ISBN: 978-1-943684-52-6 (e)

CONTENTS

My name is Donald Fart, and I'm the proud mayor of Fartville. Don't let the name fool you—this isn't some smelly, disgusting place. Sure, it's a little gassy (we are the Farts, after all). But it's a wonderful town with carefree folks. They are always relieved and feeling good. It might be the happiest place in the world.

But even happy places can go through tough times, and the tough times started with a giant Fartquake on Gas Mountain. Before I tell you the entire story about the Fartquake, let me give you a little lesson on Fartville.

Fartville resides at the base of Gas Mountain,

in the valley beneath Gas Mountain's western peak, which is called Butt-Sneeze peak. It was named after the first explorer ever to reach the top: Sir William Butt-Sneeze. He was my great, great, great granddaddy. Due to his powerful farting ability and petite frame (he was only 4 feet 11 inches) he squeezed, puffed, and poofed his way to the top, staking his flag at the peak. It was a victorious event, and it's celebrated every year to this day. Ever since then, my entire family has been in charge to keep our Fartville town brown, stinky, and crispy—just as a good Fartbody from Fartville would expect.

This mountain range, through its recycled fart vapors lying deeply within its core, has provided Fartville with the necessary gas power since . . . well, forever. It keeps the electricity on, the water running, and the entire town operating. Without it, we'd be a bunch of doomed farts in the wind. Vernon Fart, the baker, wouldn't be able to bake his famous Poof Pastries without it. Every Sunday there are lines of Fartheads waiting to scarf down his delicious Poofs to relieve their weekday stress by laying a super stinky brownish fart vapor at noon. The Fartville Toots couldn't play softball games at night, either. Every time the stinky girls tried to play they would just swallow too much air and end up with diarrhea stains in their white pinstripe knitted pants. Also, the students at Fartville Fart Academy would have to study in the dark without Gas Mountain's resources. This would not be a good thing—if they couldn't pass wind, all hope for the future would be lost. We're not the only town that relies on Gas Mountain for everything, either.

On the other end of the mountain, there's an eastern peak called Belch Peak. The town at the bottom is called Burpville. It's home to—you guessed it—the Burps.

Throughout most of our history, Fartville and Burpville have remained separate from each other. So they've existed in peace—until the Fartquake. Because sometimes nature has different plans. It's called "crap la vie," or so they say.

The morning of the Fartquake, I was following my normal routine, walking down Stink Street to City Hall. I stopped in Fartbucks for a coffee, like I always do.

"Here you go, Mayor. One Fartucinno, as usual."

"Thank you, Stacy. Beautiful day, isn't it?"

"It always is in Fartville."

"You can say that again, Stacy."

"It always is in Fartville."

"I didn't mean for you to repeat it—oh, never mind. Have a wonderful day!"

I continued on my way down Stink Street whistling my favorite tune: "Fart on My Heart" by The Gas-Passers. They were the most popular band in Fartville, and they performed every Friday night at the Fart Square. I then ran into the Police Chief—Chief Cheesecutter. He was a big fella, strong as an ox, or whatever that means. Every time I saw him, he was chugging down some fart-milk and was always carrying along his tiny Tupperware packed with his fart meals: two stinky eggs, rotten cheese, a spoonful of slim fart-tuna, and brownish fart toast.

"How are you today, Mr. Mayor?"

"Great, Chief. You're looking good. Lost weight? How's our town doing? Any trouble or mischief to report?"

"Actually, I put on five pounds of muscle. You know they say muscle burns farts—I mean, fat."

"Who says that?"

"Some Australian guy, Fartenegger. You know the one that always says, 'I'll fart back?'"

"Oh, yes, yes. And what about the town?"

"Nothing, as usual. You know, just the same old junior knuckleheads throwing stinky fart eggs through car windows. Fartville has never had any *real* trouble, and I don't think it ever will."

"I know, but we can never be too careful. That's why I always ask."

"Of course, Mr. Mayor. Oh, tell your wife I said, 'Happy Fartday.'"

"She'll be thrilled you remembered! Ciao!"

I continued along, whistling, when suddenly, a brown turd with antennas came flying towards me. Oh wait, it was a dog—a Doberman Farter. He was scared and whimpering. "What's the matter, boy?" I said, kneeling forward. But the dog just continued on past me. "Ah, he dropped a turd on my Fart Vatans!"

As I was cleaning the brownish stinky splatter from my gas loafers, I felt the ground move, which knocked me on my butt. I saw the trees shaking, the grass rumbling, and all the Fart-animals being sucked into the ground. The next thing I remember is looking up and seeing the citizens of Fartville running around in a panic, careful not to fall in the long crack that was dividing the town. They were so scared that they were farting uncontrollably. I heard trumpet farts, whistle farts, drum farts, and even silent farts. Yes, even the silent ones—oh, believe me, when a Fart farts, it's extra farty. As I was taking a whiff from the proud Farts of Fartville with my nose high to the sky, suddenly the ground stopped moving (but the farts didn't stop—weird).

Thankfully, there was very little damage to Fartville. A couple of Fart-animals fell into the cracked ground, but they'd live. They could fart themselves back up to town. Fart Square was still intact, along with most of its stores. But most importantly, no Fart-body was hurt.

Soon, I heard a loud cheer; the civilians of Fartville jumped with joy as they realized that Poof Pastries, Brown Pub (a Fartville go-to Friday night hangout), Toots, and Fart Academy were still intact. We all thought that was the end of the havoc and everything would go back to normal; but then, the next day, a group of big green-yellow, fart-ugly gremlins visited City Hall all the way from Burpville. They were giants—four Farts high.

And that was the beginning of Fartville's troubles.

The Fartquake (which the Burps called a Burpquake) did a lot more damage to Burpville than Fartville. The long mountain divide in Fartville reached all the way to Belch Peak and made it burst right open. The gas that powered Burpville was erupting into the air instead of being funneled into Burpville. They had no gas, and Burps—like Farts—can't survive without gas.

The mayor of Burpville, Dale Burp, arrived with a group of Burpville leaders. I was eager to greet our neighbors from the other side of the mountain because we rarely see each other.

Little did I know, they had their own plans the whole time.

"Mayor Fart," said Mayor Burp. "The quake has destroyed Burpville! Yet I see it hasn't damaged Fartville much."

"Luck of the Farts, I guess." I smiled. He didn't. None of them did.

"I see that you still have plenty of gas to power your town. The mountain is even *extra* gassy around here."

"You have too much gas!" one of the other Burp leaders yelled.

"Quit hogging it all!" another Burp shouted.

"Friends," I said. "There is no need for anger. We are happy to share our gas with you."

Burps were known for being grumpy. After all, Burps came from indigestion, which isn't comfortable. But Farts were made to relieve, so we were always in a good mood.

Mayor Burp continued, "We think that's a wise move, Mayor Fart. After all, we wouldn't want to fight you for it."

I laughed; I thought he was making a joke. "Farters are not fighters. We prefer to live in gassy harmony with our neighbors."

"Good to hear," Mayor Burp said. "*Very* good to hear. We shall return tomorrow to work out a plan. In the meantime, Mayor Fart, sleep well."

The rest of the Burps chuckled after he said this. I didn't think anything of it at the time; I just thought Burps had a weird sense of humor. After all, they were known to have Burp Acid—it runs in their genes.

The next day, I was walking out of Fartbucks with my usual farty skinny Fartaccino when my deputy mayor, Willard Fart, rushed over to me. He was a big fat Fart, the size of two big butts farting the best potent farts a Burpville resident could ever imagine. He could barely catch his breath—he wasn't used to running.

"Mayor . . ."

"What is it, Willard?" I said.

"The Burps! They're coming!"

"I know, Willard. We spoke about it yesterday."

"No!" he said, grabbing me by the shoulders. "They're coming *with an army.*"

I quickly ran to the top of the tallest building in Fartville—Buttblast Tower. Willard stayed below, bent at the waist in his fart position trying to catch his breath.

What I saw shocked me. There was Mayor Burp marching toward Fartville, and following behind him was every citizen of Burpville. They were armed with Burp cannons, Burp bombs, and gas grenades. Scariest of all was a sight that I couldn't believe. Behind the front lines of the Burp army were giants. They were Burps as big as houses. They were greenish-yellow in color, and I could smell their odor from where I stood.

"Monster Burps," Willard yelled, seeing the army through the corner of Buttblast. I looked down and saw he was trembling with fear. "The legends *are* true!"

They weren't coming to share Gas Mountain with us; they were coming to take over Fartville. Willard kept yelling from below, "What do we do? What do we do?"

"I don't know," I yelled back. Fartville has never had to prepare for a battle before. Ever. "We need to get to Police Chief Cheesecutter. *Now.*"

When I got down, I ran to the police precinct, with Willard far behind, wobbling and trying to catch up. I soon told Police Chief Cheesecutter what was happening. He panicked. "Oh, dear. This is terrible news," he said, letting out a squeaky, nervous fart. It's not good when your police chief is as frightened as you.

Soon I was running alongside the police chief towards the Fart Bell. "Hey, Deputy Willard! Turn around, you big lug; you're going the wrong way," Chief Cheescutter yelled as we lapped Willard still trying to make it to the station.

"This Fart Bell hasn't been rung in centuries. Maybe they're just playing a practical joke on us?" he said, worried. He continued, "Maybe they weren't real Monster Burps. Maybe they were just a bunch of Burps standing on each other in a costume."

"This isn't a joke," I said. "And those *are* real Monster Burps. They are coming to attack us."

"Oh dear," the police chief said.

The bell was rung from the police station. At first, the Fartville folks stood around, confused. Most of them had never heard the emergency alarm before, but by then the alarm didn't matter. They all started running when the Monster Burps came stomping through.

The Burps soon rampaged through town. They stampeded through Fart Square and crushed all the Fart mom-and-pop boutiques on the strip. Next, they invaded different villages burping and blowing hot lava smelly burp acid *ooze rings* from their breaths. The good Farts of Fartville buckled at their knees as they were chased away from their homes.

"Run!" I yelled into the Farty Horn speaker to everyone passing me. "Head to the Butt-Cave! *Head to the Butt-Cave!*"

The Monster Burps were unstoppable, crushing buildings with single burps that were as loud as sirens. "Blaaaah, burrrrrp, bloooorrrpt." Burp bombs were blowing up streets and landmarks, making the air smell like three-bean chili.

There were Pizza Burps and Soda Burps, Taco Burps and Cheeseburger Burps, high-pitched burps, low-pitched burps—burps of each and every kind. They were taking over Fartville.

I stood there, waving my citizens past me. The marauding Burp army approached.

Walking over to me out of the destruction was Mayor Burp. He was smiling. He stopped in front of me and raised his hand. The entire army stopped, looking down. The only sounds heard were the screams of Farts heading out of town.

"So, here we are, Mayor Fart. Or should I even call you that?" He looked around and the damage he and his Burps had caused. "You seem to be the mayor of nothing right now."

Evil laughs echoed through the army. I seemed to be the only one who didn't find it funny. Burps have a weird sense of humor. As much as I wanted to punch Mayor Burp in his smelly mouth, I couldn't. I was outnumbered. It was a whole Burp army versus Deputy Willard and I. Oh, wait—Willard had wobbled to the Butt-Cave. It was just me.

So I made the smart move instead. I raised my hand, and the entire Burp army looked up. Then I lowered my hand. Their eyes hit the floor. Then I raised my hand and let out the loudest, smelliest, ear-popping fart. It made even the giant Burps bend over at the waist.

POOF!

I turned around and jetted to join my fellow Farts in the Butt-Cave. There were some things we had to figure out—and fast.

All of Fartville was now huddled together in the Butt-Cave. Every Fart was scared and rattled to their core. Loud Farts, quiet Farts, long Farts, and short Farts—the Butt-Cave was holding them all in.

They all looked onto the territory they called home. The Burps had overrun it. They were already occupying our parks, landmarks, office buildings, and homes. They even started refurnishing. It was the worst day in Fartville history.

And I was mayor when it happened. I knew I had to do something. We had to rally ourselves together, against all odds.

"We'll never rally against these odds!" Willard Fart said, which was of no help. Others in the crowd agreed.

"Yeah!"

"He's right!"

"The odds are too great!"

"It's dark in here!"

"We're in a cave, dummy!"

If I hadn't stepped in, the Farts would have all turned against each other. It was time to reclaim our town as one force. Many Farts together can blow away any challenger . . . I think. Now all I had to do was convince them. I got up on a big turd in the Butt-Cave and addressed them. "Good Farts of Fartville, lend me your ears!"

They ignored me.

"Friends, please, listen!"

They continued arguing.

I then reached deep down and let out the biggest, loudest fart I could. The epic toot echoed through the cavern. Finally, everyone stopped and listened.

"Generations of Farts have inhabited Fartville. Our mothers and fathers, their mothers and fathers, and their mothers and fathers—back to the first Farts who ever farted in this direction. We cannot let Burps or anyone take what's rightfully ours."

Rings of "Yes!" and "He's right!" were heard from the crowd, along with one "I'm hungry," which I think came from Willard.

"We need a plan," I said.

"I have a plan!" a mysterious voice spoke out.

Others in the crowd turned to see who it was. Walking from the back was Rumbly Fart. He was the toughest Fart in town and was one of the only Farts ever to venture through Gas

Mountain. He'd seen more of the world outside of Fartville than anyone else. When he farted, people listened.

"Those Burps out there, they got monsters, don't they? Well, all we need are some monsters of our own to fight back."

There was silence. The Farts looked at each other, confused.

I spoke up. "Rumbly Fart, there are no Monster Farts. Those are just old Farty tales."

"You didn't believe Monster Burps existed either," he responded. "But look at what's running all over our town right now." The crowd murmured, realizing Rumbly Fart had a point.

"Besides," he added, "I seen 'em with my own eyes!"

A gasp came from the crowd.

"How come you never mentioned this before?" Willard asked him.

"Because no one ever asked me."

The crowd murmured again—another good point.

"Our Monster Farts live deep down in the belly of the mountain. But they don't release on their own, no sir. You got to wake 'em up!"

"So, Rumbly Fart," I said, "you're saying that someone needs to go into the dark and deep parts of the mountain? Deeper than any Fart alive has ever been before and wake up the Monsters?"

"That's about the long and the short of it, yep. I'm happy to go because I know how to get most of the way there. But I'm not very friendly, so they might not like me."

Rumbly Fart's sheer confidence left me with little choice. Plus, I wanted to get re-elected. "I will join you, Rumbly Fart. I will speak to these Monster Farts."

"Sh-should I go with you, boss?" Willard asked, hoping I would say no.

I did. "It will only be Rumbly Fart and I. The fewer people, the better; time is of the essence. Our homes are at stake. We must be quick."

With torches lit, the other Farts wished Rumbly Fart and I luck. I took a deep breath and followed Rumbly into the tunnel leading to the center of Gas Mountain.

I felt like we had been walking for hours. Rumbly tried telling jokes to pass the time, but he only knew one joke, so he just kept repeating it.

"What do you call a Fart sleeping in strawberry jam?"

"Rumbly, I know the answer. You've told this joke like twenty times."

"Silent . . . but jelly! Ha!"

If I had to hear that awful joke once more, I would lose it. Thankfully, we finally got to our destination. The air felt different down there. It felt steamy and damp.

"Well," Rumbly said, "this is the farthest

I've been. But we're close enough to get their attention."

I gulped. The truth was, I had never been more frightened in all my life.

"Who goes there?" a deep, unseen voice said.

Rumbly was the one to speak up. "We're here to have a word with y'all. Could you come out of that dang darkness for a minute?"

Rumbly had been right; he wasn't very friendly.

"Please," I added.

A moment later, a set of eyes appeared high above us. It took everything in me not to run and hide. The eyes were looking down, examining us curiously. "What do you want?" the creature barked. He didn't sound like he wanted to be bothered.

"Listen here, big guy—"

I stopped Rumbly from saying anymore and took over the talking from there.

"Hi, Mr. Monster Fart. My name is Donald Fart. I'm the mayor of the neighboring town in Fartville. We're your little brothers and sisters."

The eyes just looked at me. The monster remained silent.

I continued. "I'm not sure if you noticed the Fartquake that happened yesterday . . ."

"Of course, I did," he thundered. "I live in the mountain, don't I?"

"Right, yes; of course. See, the thing is, the Burps from Burpville lost gas power on their side of the mountain. We offered to share our resources here, but instead, they attacked our town and took it over."

"Attacked?"

"Yes. Now all the Farts are huddled in Butt-Cave. Their homes are gone. The Burps had Monster Burps on their side, so we were wondering . . ."

"Can you help us out of this mess or not?" Rumbly interrupted.

The monster thought. "No Farts in Fartville? This . . . cannot be."

"It is, giant, sir. I assure you, it is," I said.

Suddenly, the lone sets of eyes were joined by other sets of eyes floating high in the darkness. They looked at each other and muttered to themselves, and I think they finally blinked. Rumbly and I glanced at each other while they spoke high in the sky.

A moment later, the Monster Fart we'd been talking to stepped forward. We saw him in full . . . we wished we didn't.

Fart craters occupied his face. His eyes drooped. His legs were the size of tree stumps, and he reeked of a toxic fart smell that could turn roses into weeds—instantly. The others were just like him, but shorter. They truly were monstrous Farts, bigger and smellier than any Burp, big or small.

"Let's take Fartville back for you," the leader said, followed by a rip of gas that rustled the nests off the trees. Rumbly and I almost choked.

The Monster Fart symphony was heard throughout the mountain and beyond. I was later told the Farts in the Butt-Cave clung together tightly, not knowing if the sound was another Fartquake. Then, once the smell of these farts followed the thunderous sound, they all held their noses. For a Fart to be disgusted by another Fart, it must be the most gnarly fart in the world.

Climbing through the skeleton of the mountain 'til they reached the top, the Monster Farts emerged from an opening near Butt-Sneeze

Peak. Riding on the shoulders of two of the Monster Farts were Rumbly and I.

"To Fartville!" I yelled.

"I wanted to say that!" Rumbly said.

"Go ahead, then; you can say it too." I climbed off the shoulders of the leader, Monster Pepperoni Fart. "You lead them down the mountain, Rumbly. I'll gather the others."

"All right, I will. To Fartville!"

And so the new Monster Fart army charged down the slopes of Gas Mountain and into the town. As they entered Fartville, they blew away dozens and dozens of small Burps in the way. The Burps were no match for the pure gassy power spraying in every direction. The gases passed so hard that the Burps were sent flying clear out of town; they didn't stand a chance.

The most devastating were the Burrito Monster Farts, with their combination of meat, cheese, and beans. They were clearing out entire avenues overrun with Burps. No Burp is a match for a Burrito Monster Fart.

Once the recluse Monster Farts made their way to the center of town, the town Farts that were stuck in Butt-Cave started coming out. At first, they couldn't believe their eyes when the mythical beasts stampeded past them. But once they came to grips with what they saw, they were fired up. With Monster Farts on their side, they could do anything!

That's when I reappeared and stood before them all. "Proud Farts! We found friends in the mountains! Let's join our friends and take back Fartville! What do you say?"

"For Fartville!" Willard yelled.

"For Fartville!" everyone else responded by a synchronized fart tune—"Poooit." They charged forth, screaming into town.

They might have entered Butt-Cave as a frightened group, but they were now leaving Butt-Cave as an army, ready to take back their homes. We met with Rumbly and the Monster Farts on Stink Street just down the road from the remaining Burps.

"Let's end this once and for all," I said.

"You keep taking all the cool lines!" Rumbly complained.

"Sorry," I said. "Say a cool line now."

Rumbly hummed and hawed trying to think of one. "Let's, er . . . let's get those stupid Burps out of here!"

It wasn't a very cool line.

As we came down Stink Street toward City Hall, the Monster Burps were just sitting around the fountain. They were arguing in pacts with Mayor Burp and the other Burp leaders. "Buuuuurrrrp, baaaaap, booooo—aaaa—phhhttt." They couldn't figure out how to divide up Fartville amongst themselves. Little did they know their army was being destroyed on Stink Street.

"Okay, okay," a frustrated Mayor Burp snapped. "From Squeak Street to SBD Boulevard is Monster town, and from Butt-Ripple Road to Bowel Avenue is Little Burpville!"

"Clear-The-Room Avenue," the Monster Cheese Burp insisted.

The flying Burp smells from all directions got everyone screaming and yelling at each other again. I cleared my throat to get their attention. It didn't work. Monster Fart then quickly stomped the ground and all but Willard had to get their bearings. They all turned and looked at us, surprised and confused.

"Well, well, Mayor Fart, looks like you got some—whaaaa?" Before Mayor Burp could finish his sentence, Monster Burger Fart rushed towards Mayor Burp, lifted him up, and tossed him over City Hall. Mayor Burp screamed through the air until a thump shut him up.

Once this happened, two of the Monster Burps attacked Monster Burger Fart, but Monster Anchovy Fart stepped between them, bent over, and let out a fart that knocked both the Monster Burps out cold. The burpy gasses that came out of Monster Burp's mouth bounced back off the wave of the fart gas and knocked out all the smaller Burps in the army behind them.

The remaining Monster Burps now looked at the Monster Fart and the Fartville team standing before them. They knew they had no chance. So they turned on their own army by tying up the knocked out Burp leaders. "Hey, what do you say guys—truce?" said one of the feeble Burp soldiers.

At that moment, a battered Mayor Burp came out of hiding behind the remaining Burp soldiers. We all looked at him.

"Hehe," he said. "Yeah, good idea; how about a truce?"

Rumbly Fart walked over and grabbed Mayor Burp. "I'll show you a truce, you little—"

"Stop, Rumbly," I said. "We will put Mayor Burp and the other Burp leaders in jail before we decide what to do with them. They betrayed us, but that doesn't mean the rest of the Burp citizens have to suffer because of what Mayor Burp told them to do."

The Burps who overheard this were surprised. One of them even yelled at Mayor Burp, and even I could smell the hot anchovies from afar. "You told us the Farts were evil and didn't want to help us!"

"You lied!" another one added. Flustered,

Mayor Burp whistled a "𝔹𝕦𝕣𝕣 ... 𝕣𝕣 ... 𝕣𝕡𝕥." Busted! Even the remaining Monster Burp soldiers looked down at him in anger.

"Um, hehe. Fellow Burps, I was just trying to do what was best for—"

One of his own Monster Burps picked him and tossed him into a jail cell at the police hall.

"Couldn't have done it better myself," Police Chief Cheesecutter commented.

Another remaining Burp leader named Garlic Burp spoke up. He appeared cool and suave but was a bit greasy. "We were mistaken, Farts. We did a terrible thing to your town. We are sorry. Our city of Burpville was destroyed, and we had nowhere to go. Instead of taking up your generous offer, we attacked you. Can you ever forgive us?"

Many of the Farts were angry and wanted to punish them all, but I spoke up.

"We cannot send you back to Burpville," I said. "There is nothing for you there. And yes, you did attack us, which will take a long time to forgive. But Farts are honest people who want to help. We can build on lands right outside of Fartville that you can call home, and you can share our power from Gas Mountain until we get Belch Peak sealed."

Both Burps and Farts were shocked at the offer. Then Rumbly Fart put his hand on my shoulder. "It's the right thing to do, boss," he said.

"Oh, thank you, Mayor Fart!" Garlic Burp said. All the other Burps were just as grateful and excited, burping in the background. Garlic Burp then added, "We will sign a peace treaty promising that we will never attack the honest people of Fartville ever again."

"Good, good," I said. But where was all the

. . . .

press when I needed them? This was prime time coverage. Geez!

Cheers came from everywhere. But the cheering was cut short—tremors were running through the ground again. At first we thought it was another Fartquake, but when we all turned to the mountain, we were stunned at what we saw.

They were gooey, slimy, and green. Some were thick and fat and some were fluid and thin. Fartville had a new invader—one we had never seen in these parts before. Yikes!

"The Boogers are coming," Rumbly cried.

"Fart help us all," Willard whispered.

(to be continued)

ABOUT THE AUTHOR

A.M. Shah is an author of several picture and chapter books as well as the MONSTER FART WARS series. When he is not reading and writing dense briefs that make his eyeballs splash out of his sockets during law school, he is writing fun fiction for kids. He lives with his wife Melissa and their two boogers Ashton and Ashley.

OTHER COOL DUDE BOOKS
BY A.M. SHAH

FARTS VS. BURPS

Deputy Mayor Willard

Mayor Donald Fart

Police Chief Cheesecutter

Rumbly Fart

Cheeseburger Burp

Taco Burp

Pizza Burp

Monster Fart

Dale Burp

Garlic Burp

Monster Burp

Check out . . .

MONSTER
ZOMBIES
Are
Coming for Johnny

A.M. SHAH
illustrated by Pedro Demetriou

Made in the USA
San Bernardino, CA
13 January 2018